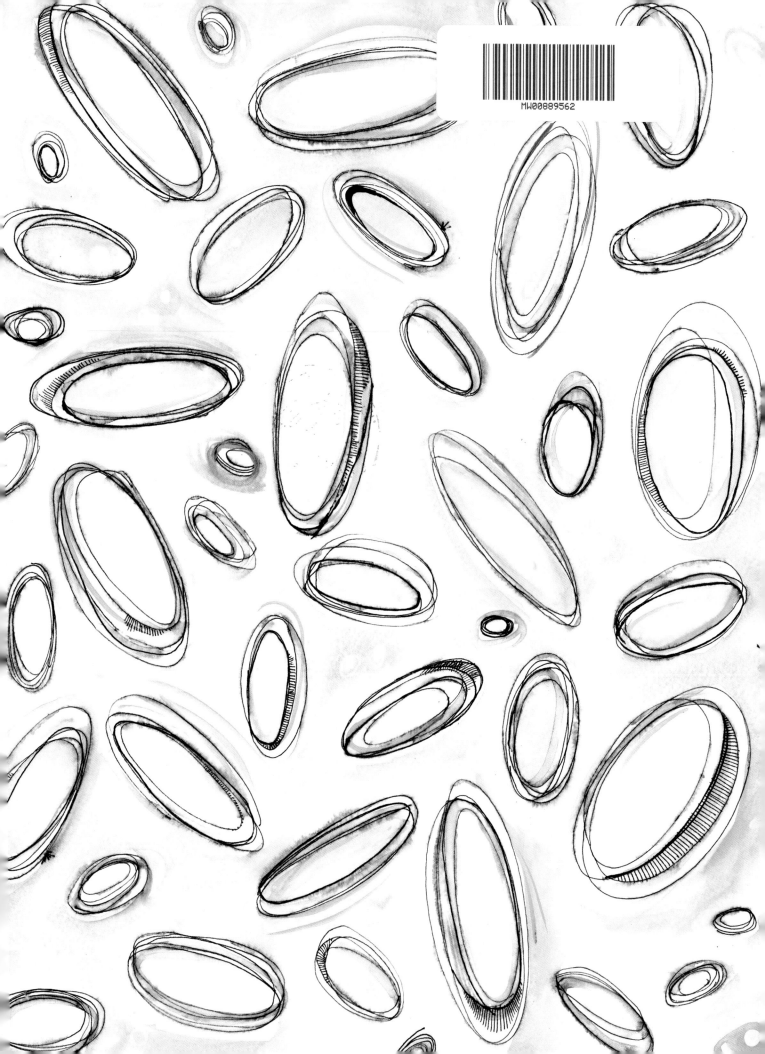

MEG'S LITTLE FREE LIBRARY
ALWAYS FOR FREE
CHARTER 12C849
NEVER FOR SALE
@MEGSLFLI20849

Dizzy the Mutt with the Propeller Butt

By Ian Punnett

Illustrated By D.C. Ice

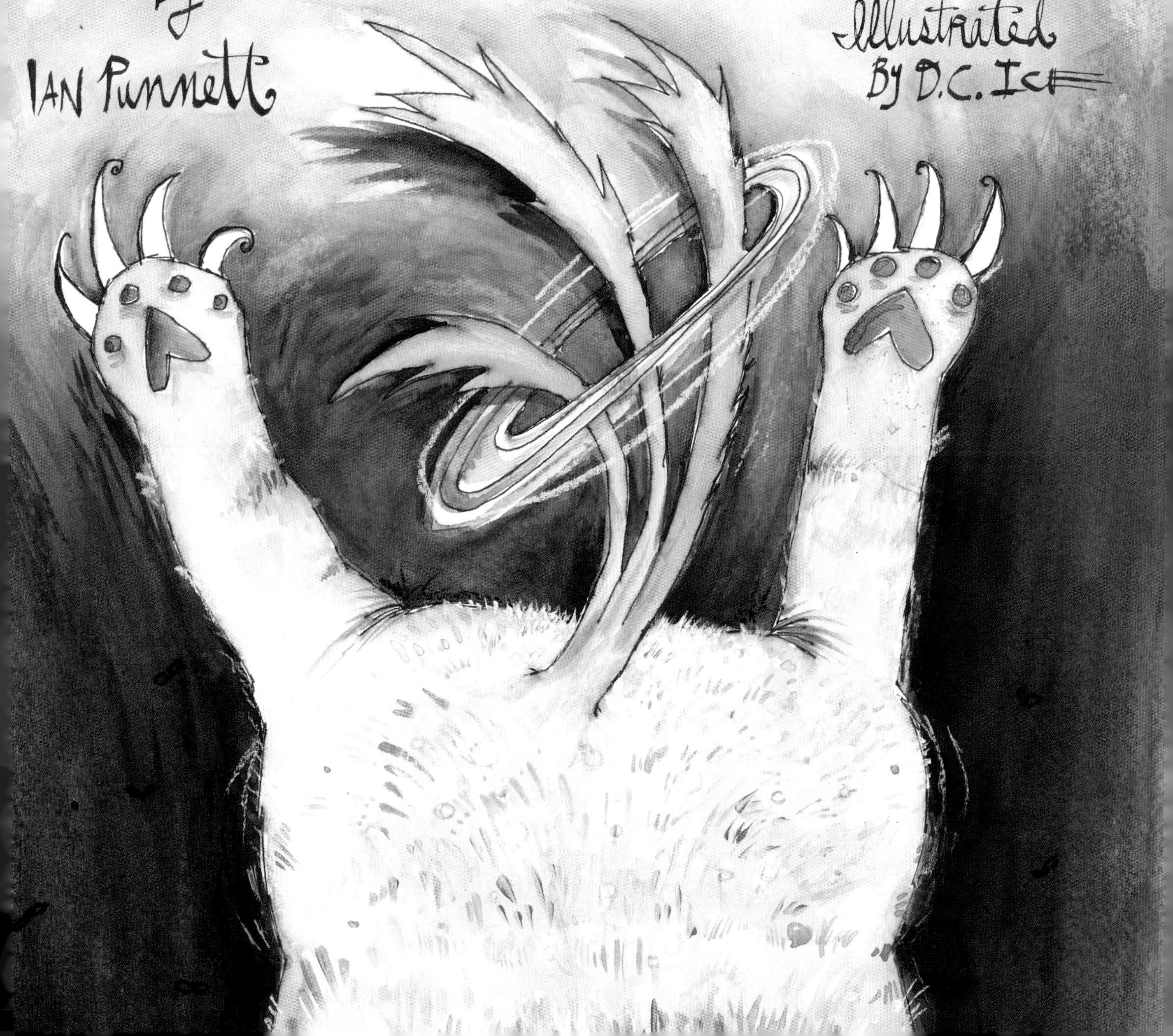

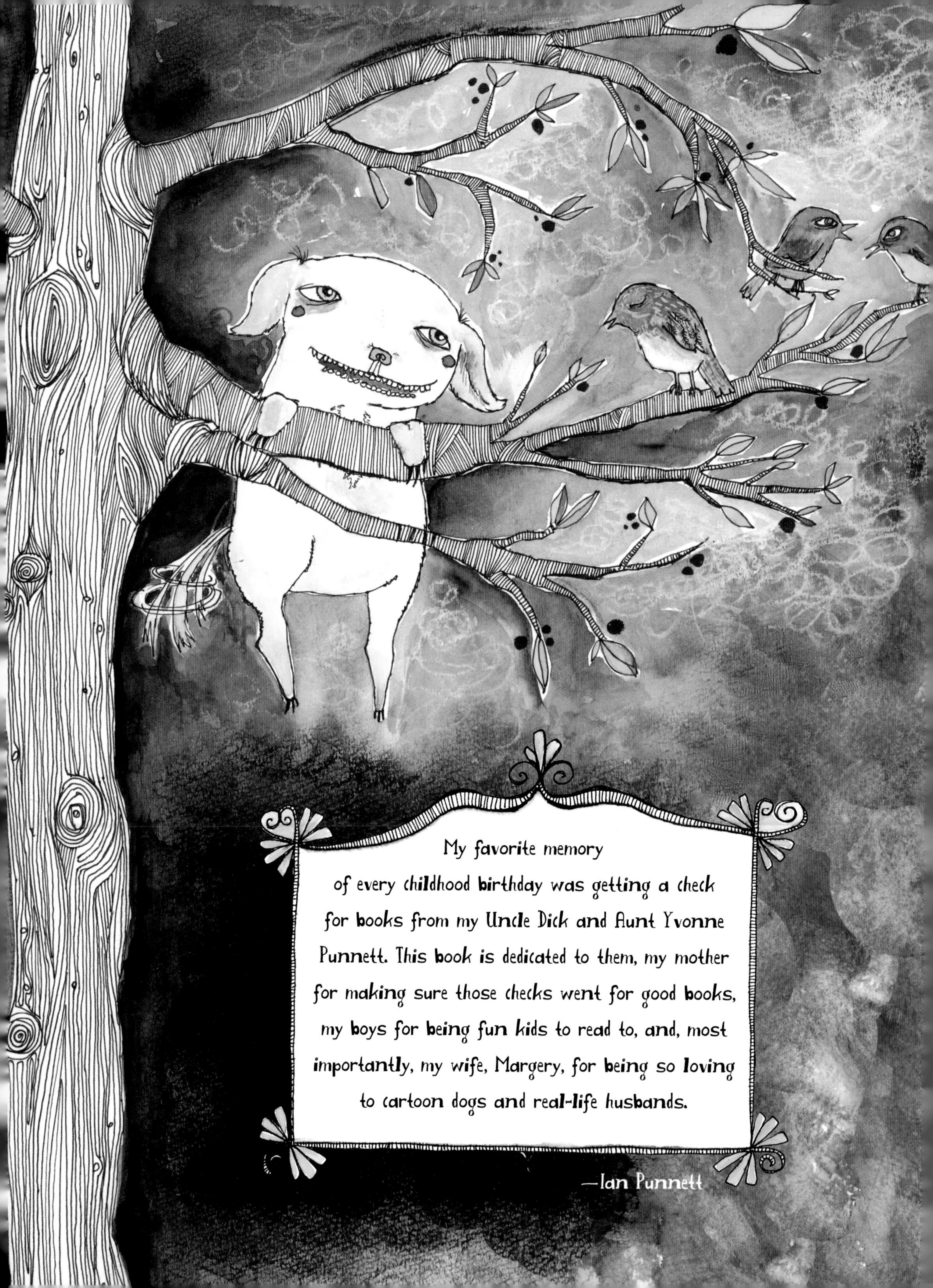

My favorite memory
of every childhood birthday was getting a check
for books from my Uncle Dick and Aunt Yvonne
Punnett. This book is dedicated to them, my mother
for making sure those checks went for good books,
my boys for being fun kids to read to, and, most
importantly, my wife, Margery, for being so loving
to cartoon dogs and real-life husbands.

—Ian Punnett

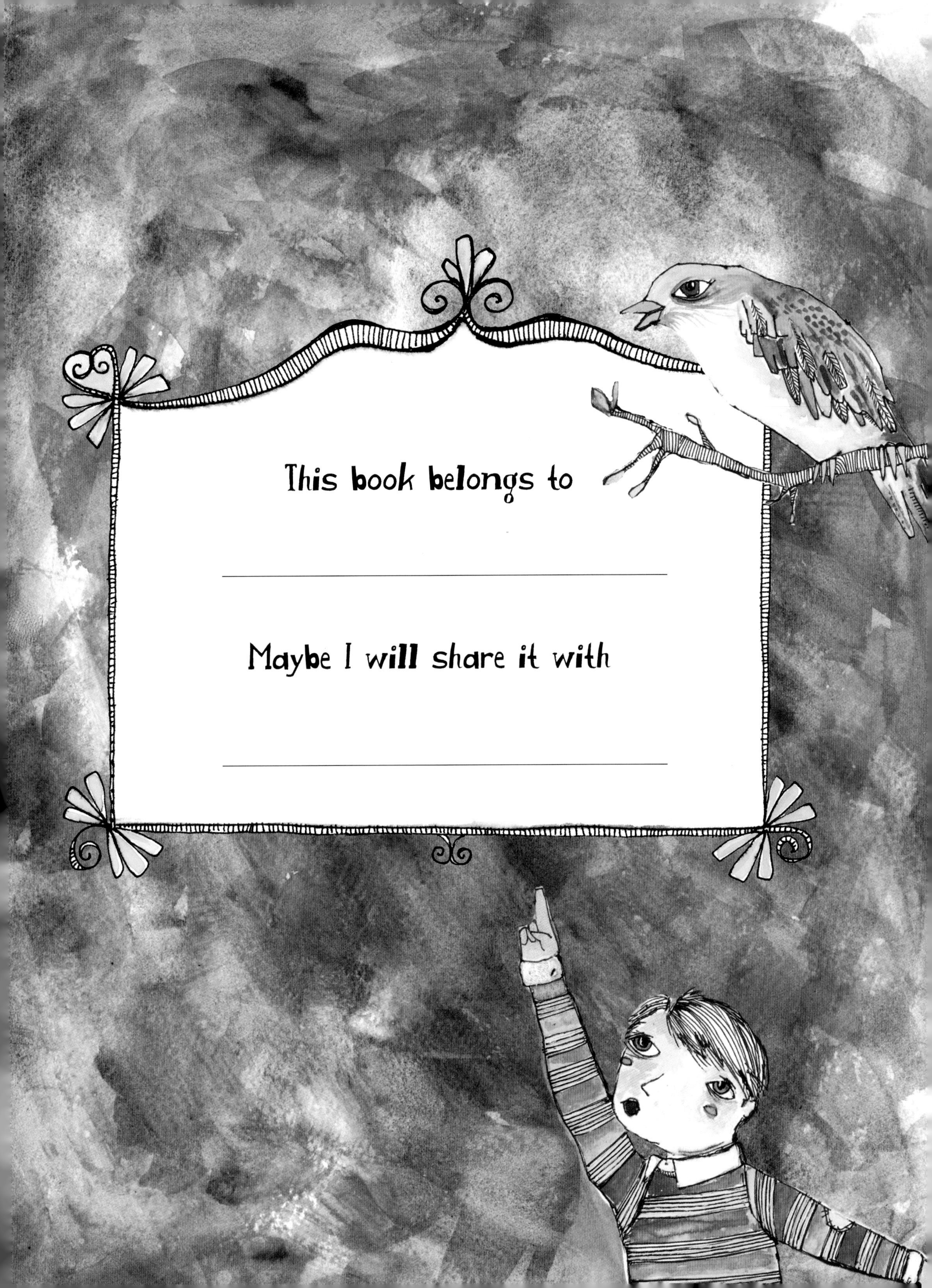
This book belongs to
Maybe I will share it with

This is the history,
with a bit of a mystery,
of a dog that confuses me so.

This book is about
a dog that gets out.
How? Well, maybe *you'll* know.

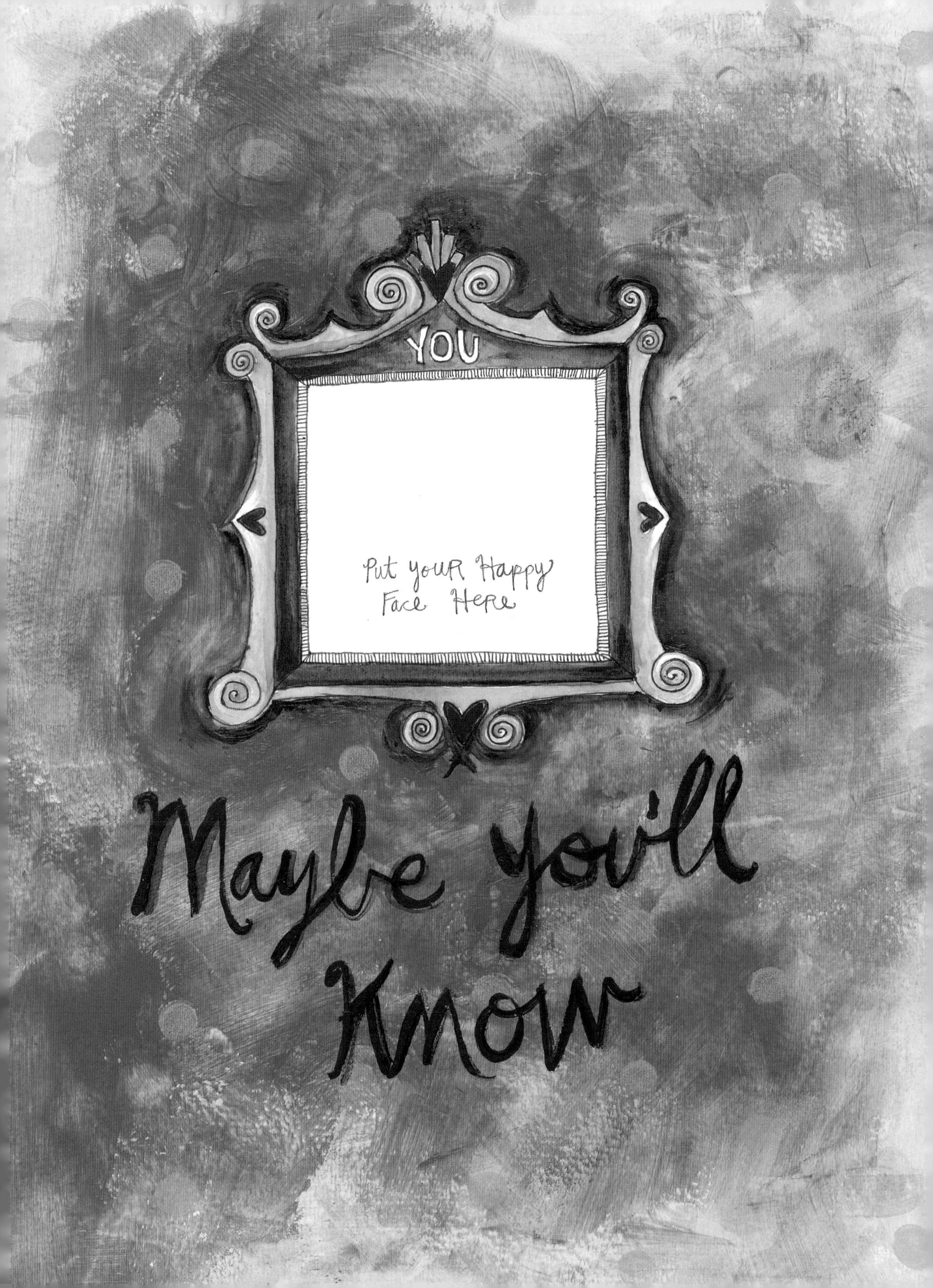
YOU
Put YOUR Happy Face Here
Maybe you'll Know

It started one morning
when, quite without warning,
Mom shouted, "We need a new pet!"

At the shelter sat Dizzy.
What kind of dog is he?
That's something we **still** don't know yet.

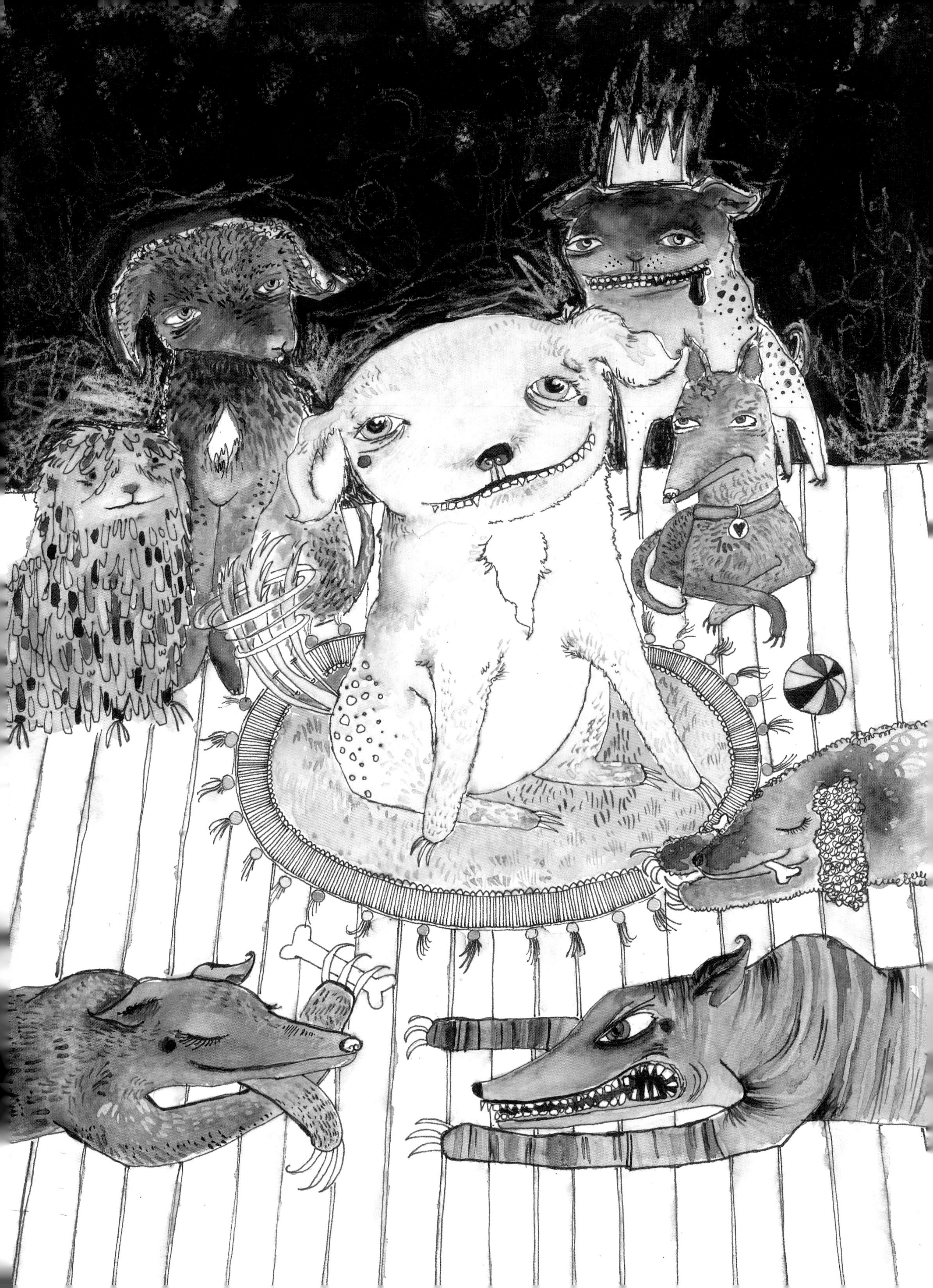

By the way that he licked us,
we're glad that he picked us.
This mutt we were **lucky to buy!**

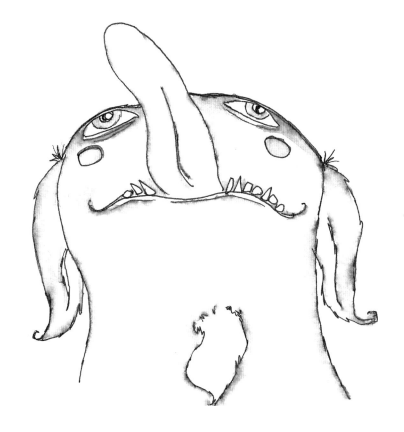

As we walked down the street,
I thought his **back** feet
were hovering as if he could **fly!**

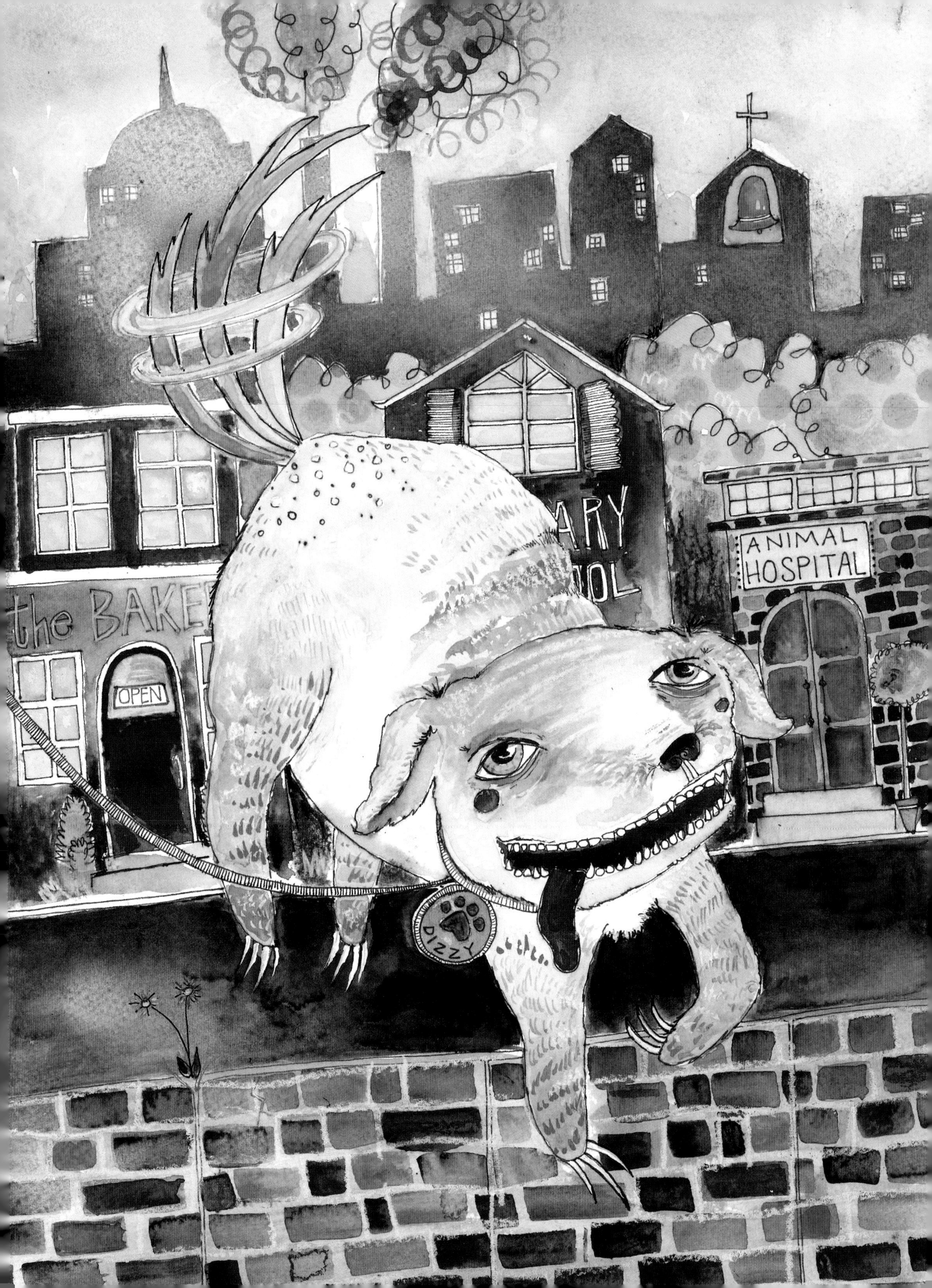

the BAKE
OPEN
ARY
OL
ANIMAL
HOSPITAL
DIZZY

After scratching my noodle,
I guessed, "He's part poodle,
but the back half is kind of a puzzle."

So we took Dizzy uptown
and showed him around.
"Does anyone know for-shuzzle?"

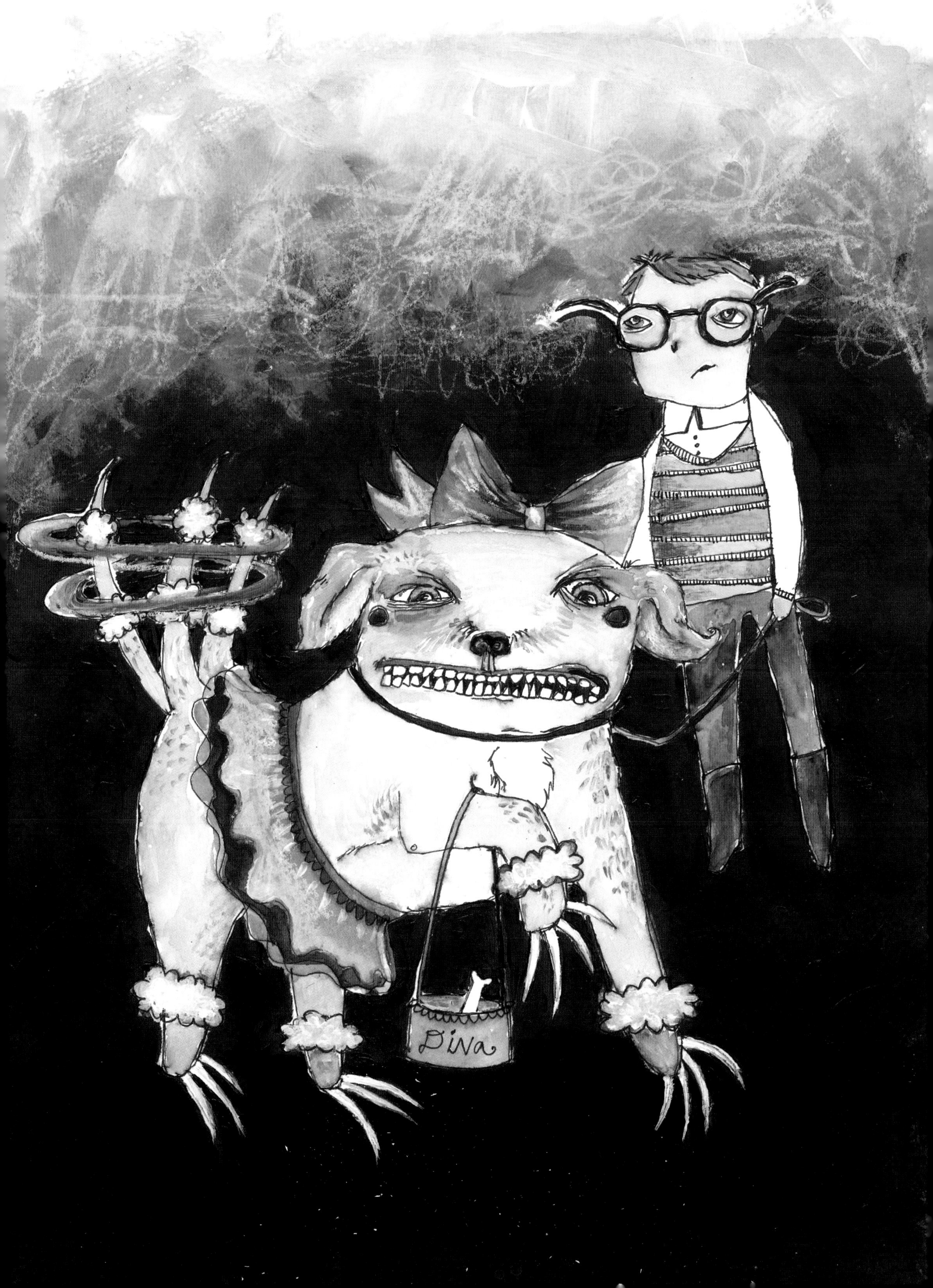
Dina

"Part frog and part poodle—
that would make him a froodle!"
muttered a man who was pushing a broom.

"No! Part rooster, part poodle—
a cocker-doodle-doodle!"
said a maid who was dusting a room.

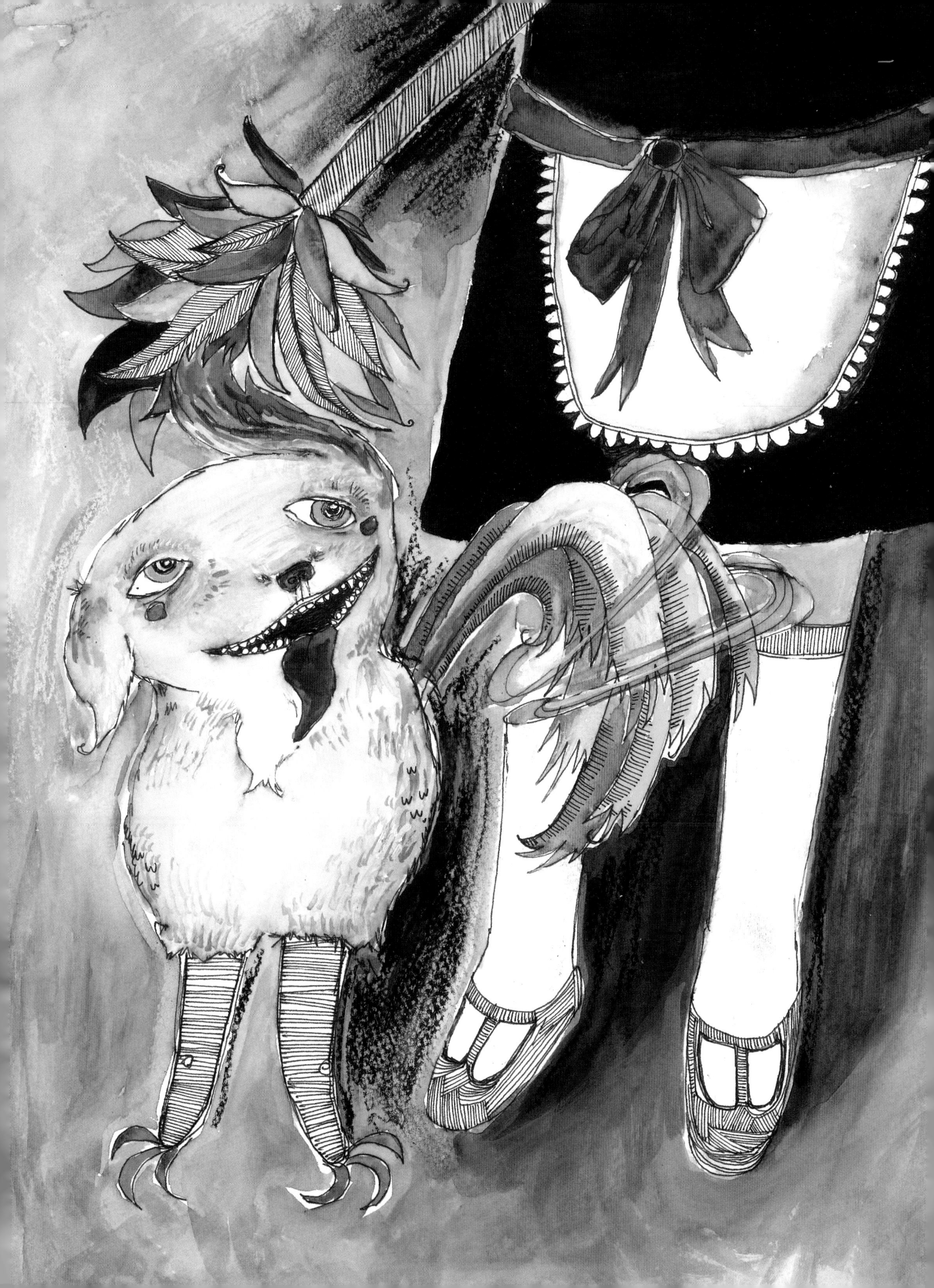

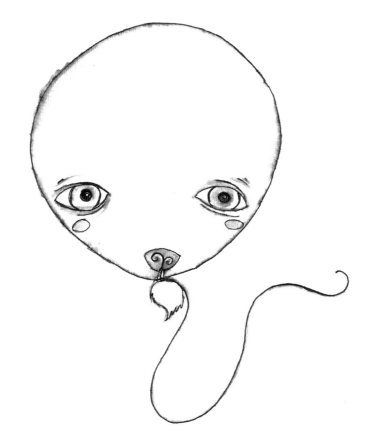

"Part **balloon**, part poodle—
a rare breed of **balloodle**!"
cracked a guy whose name tag read, "Billy."

My kids told a whopper.
They said, "He's part 'copter!"
Helicopter! Now isn't that silly?

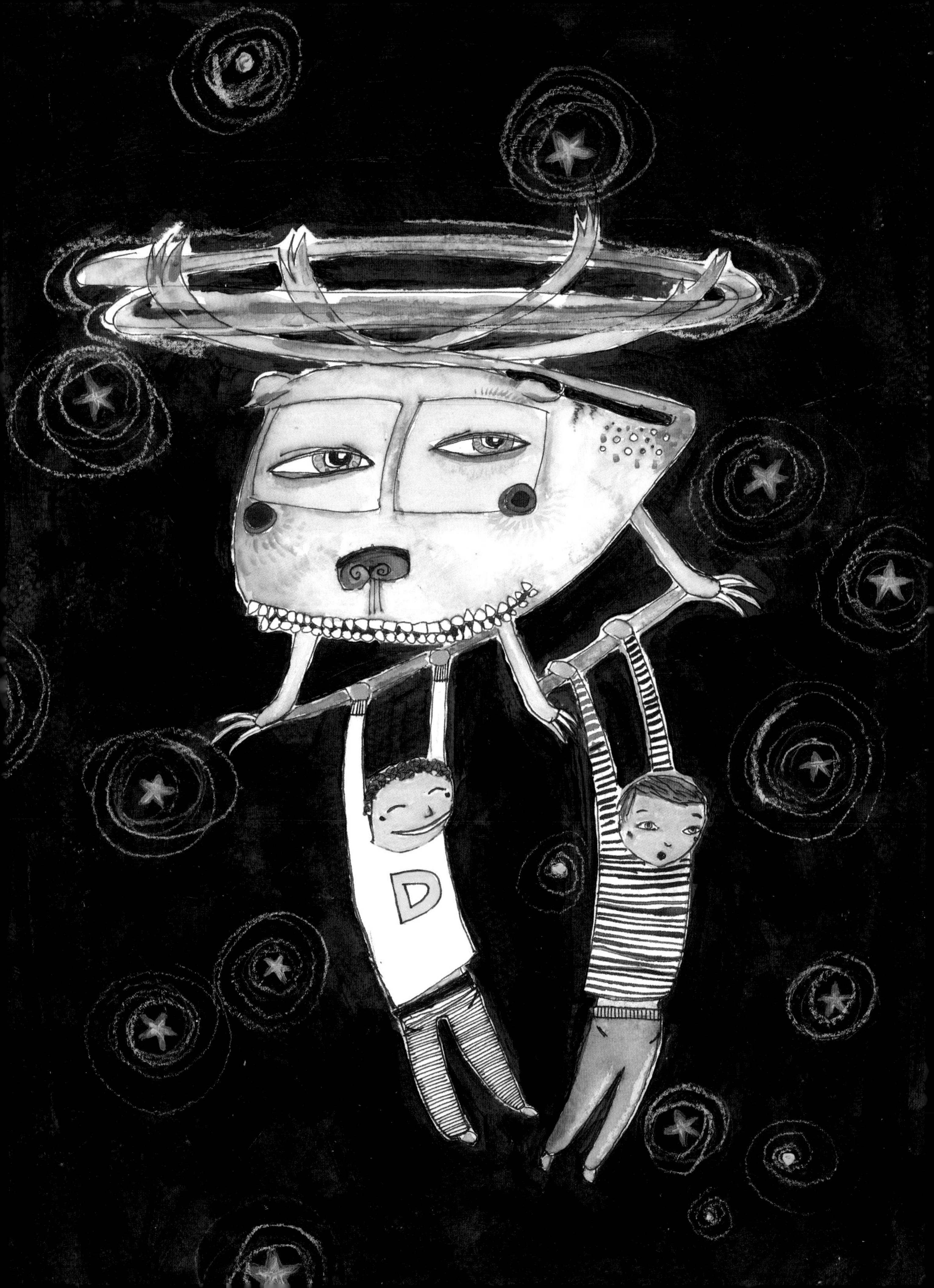

Around his new home
little Dizzy did roam,
sniffing every inch, nook, and cranny.

He loved his new life,
especially my wife,
my two boys, and even their granny.

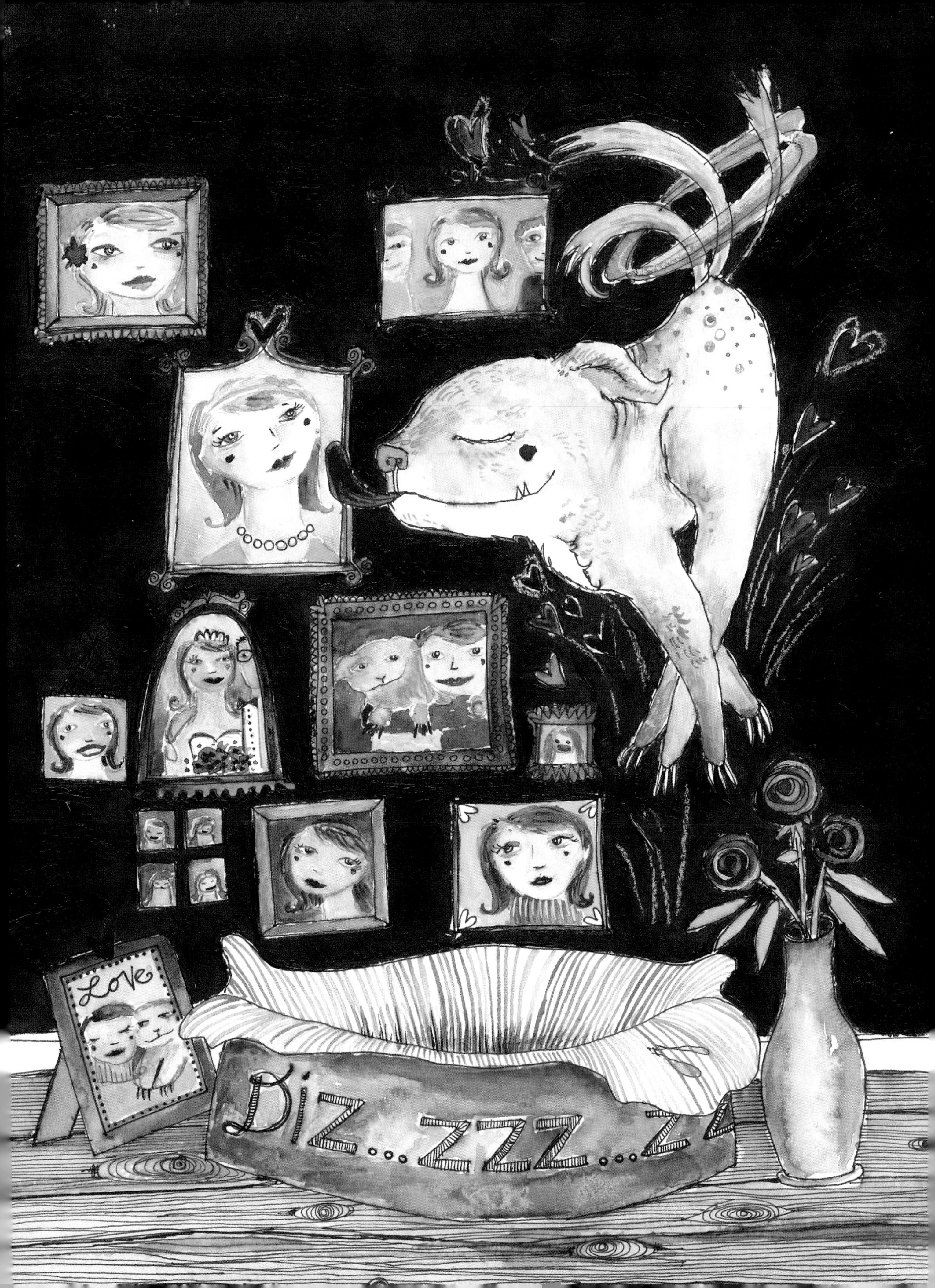
Love
Diz...zzz...z

Now, this part seems braggy,
but his tail was so waggy
he couldn't have been happier more.

And this may seem nutty,
but I swear our new buddy
was raising his butt off the floor!

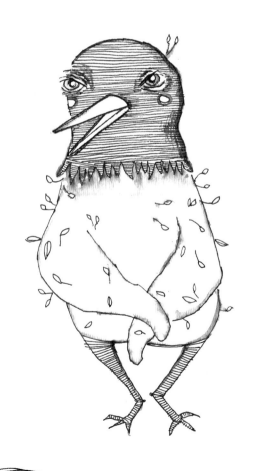

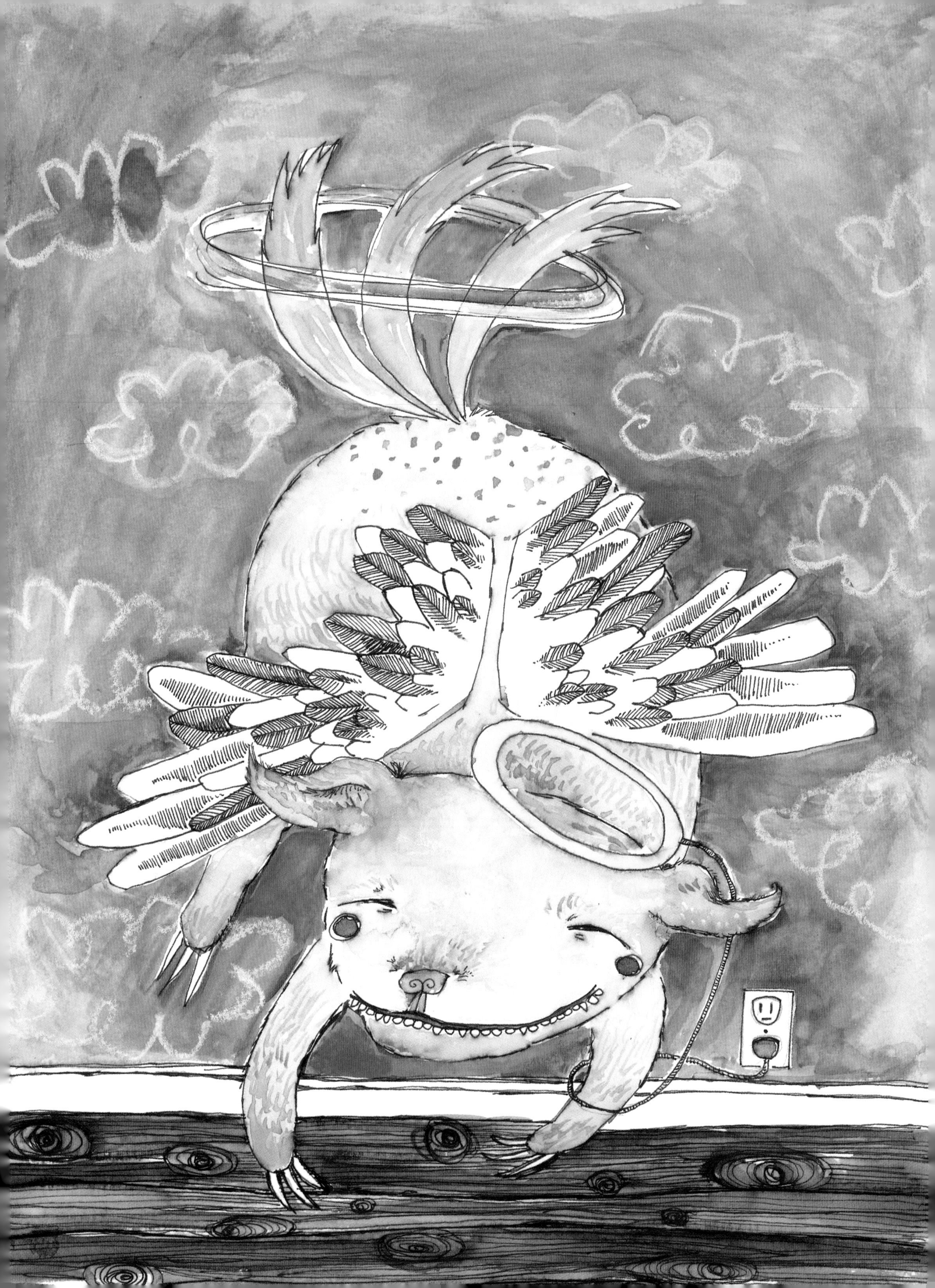

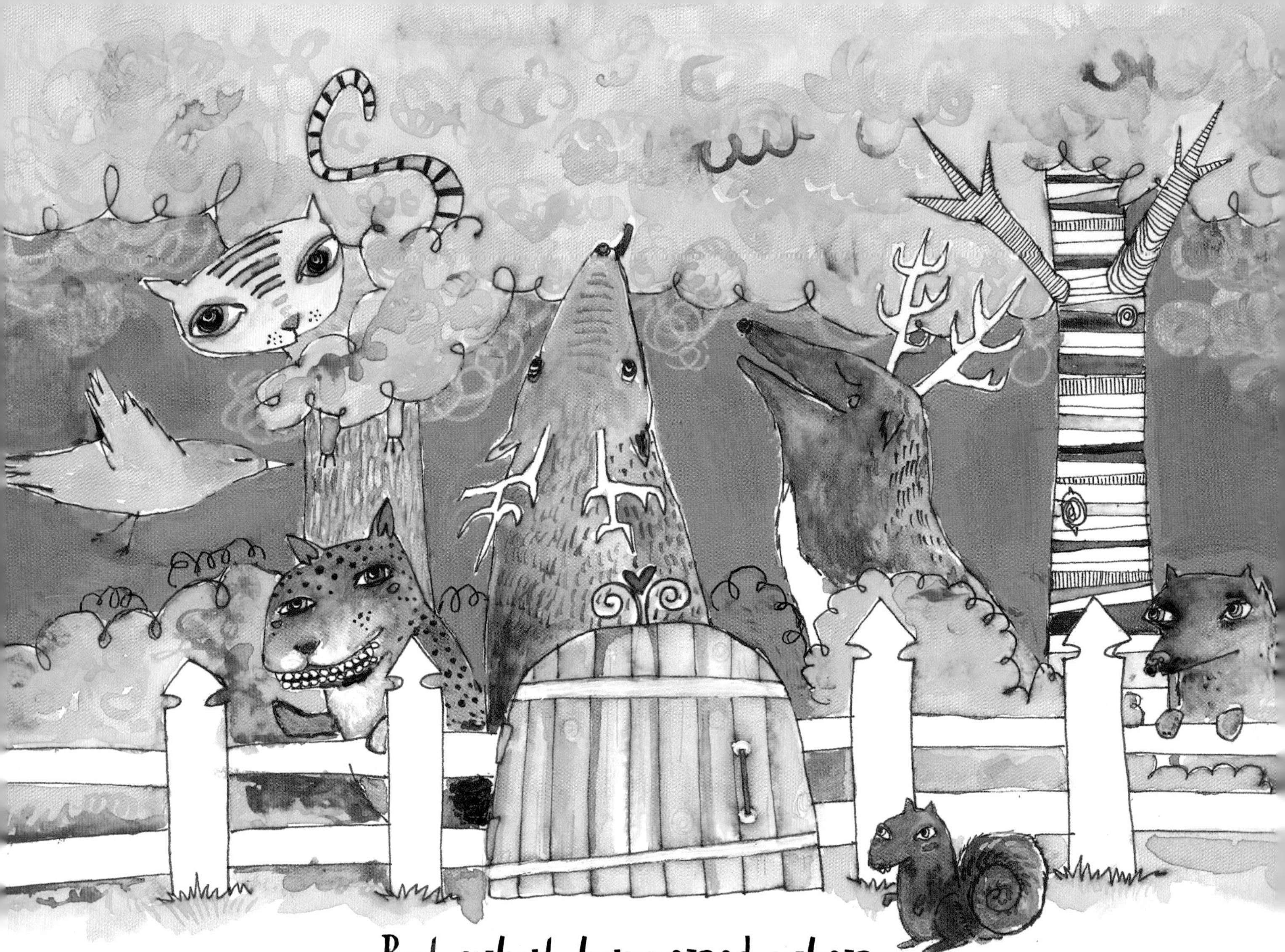

But what happened when
Dizzy was put in his pen
is every dog owner's worst fear.

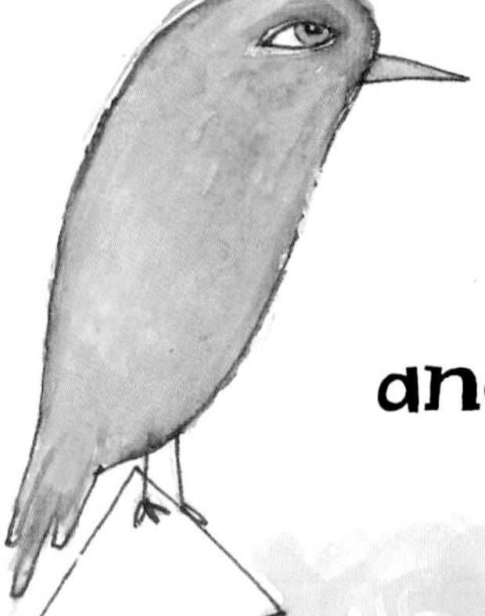

Not five minutes went by,
then I heard a faint cry
and when I looked up, he'd disappeared.

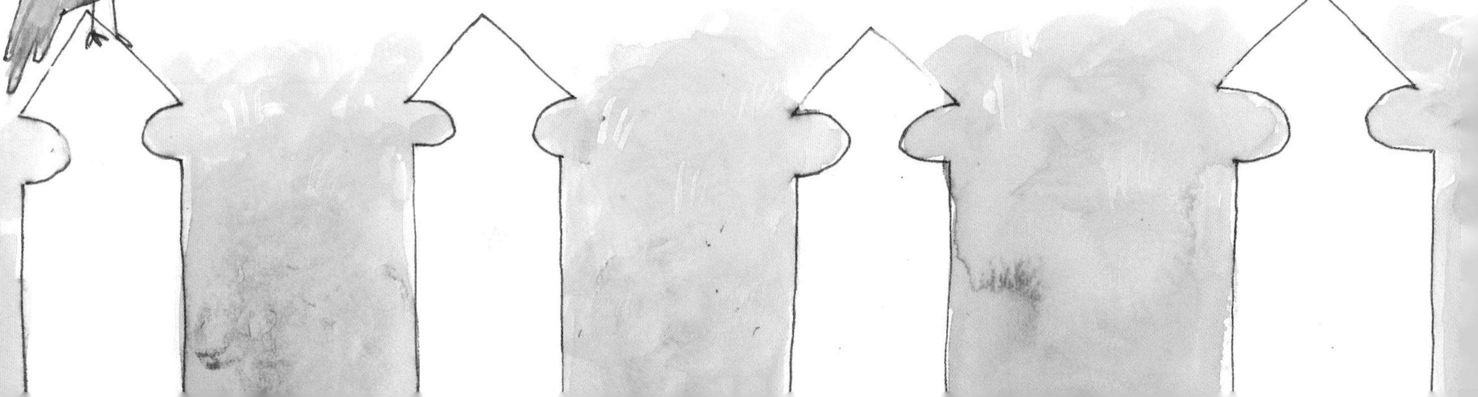

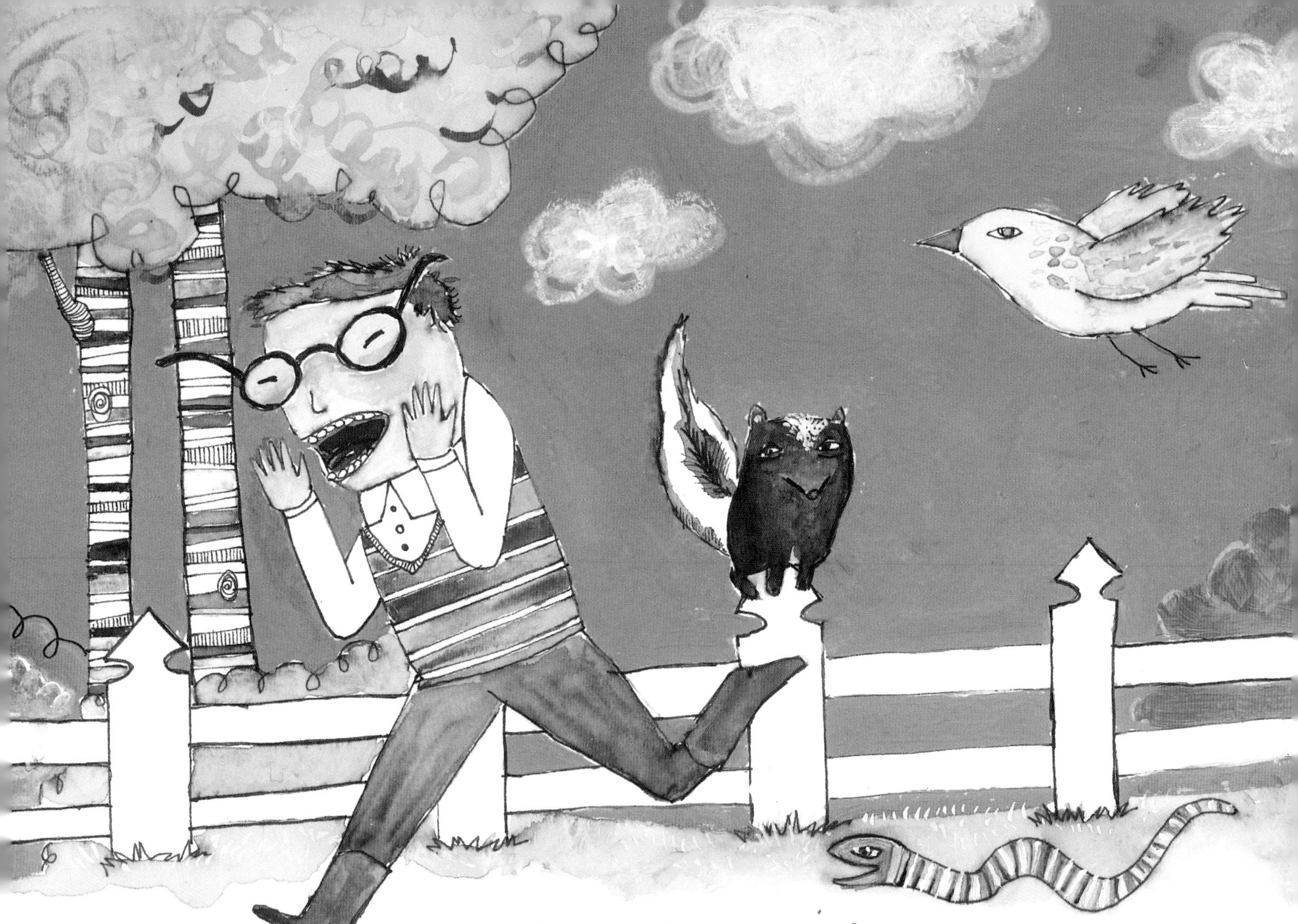

I ran through the yard.
Could he have gone very far?
Could he have jumped over the old wooden gate?

He must have been busy,
our little dog Dizzy,
to have made such a perfect escape.

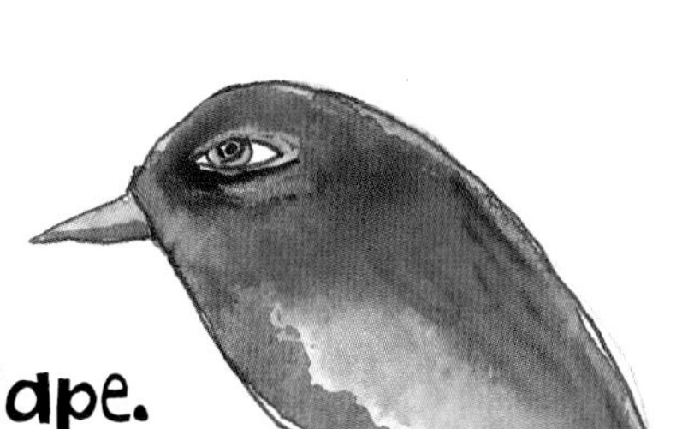

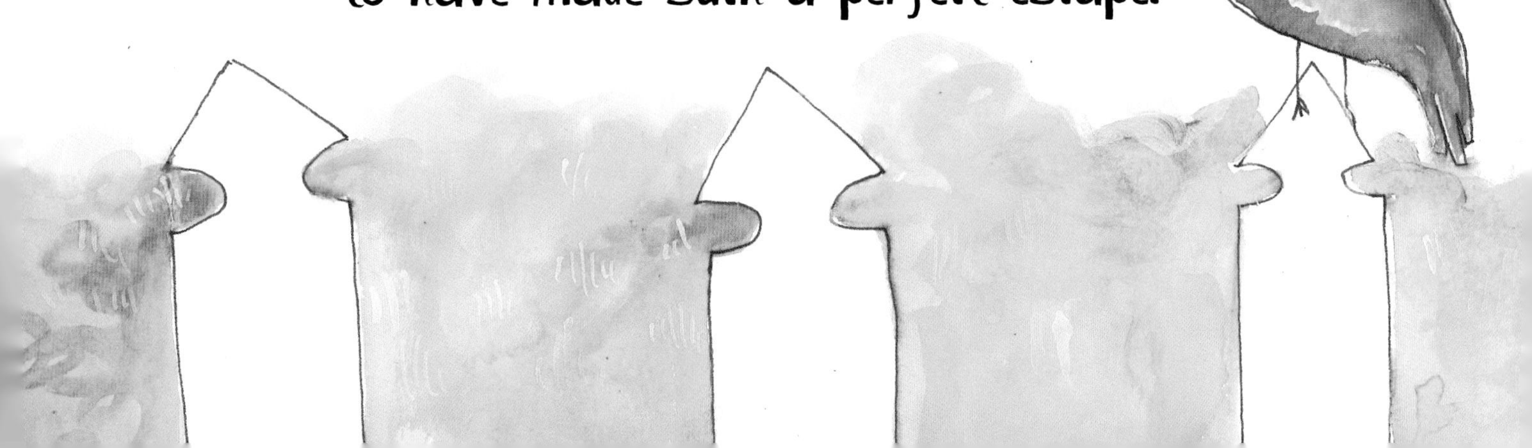

Could this dog be part mole?
Did he dig a quick hole?
Tunneled out? And if so, tell me where!

But then, from the roof,
I heard a loud "woof."
Hey! How'd he get up there?

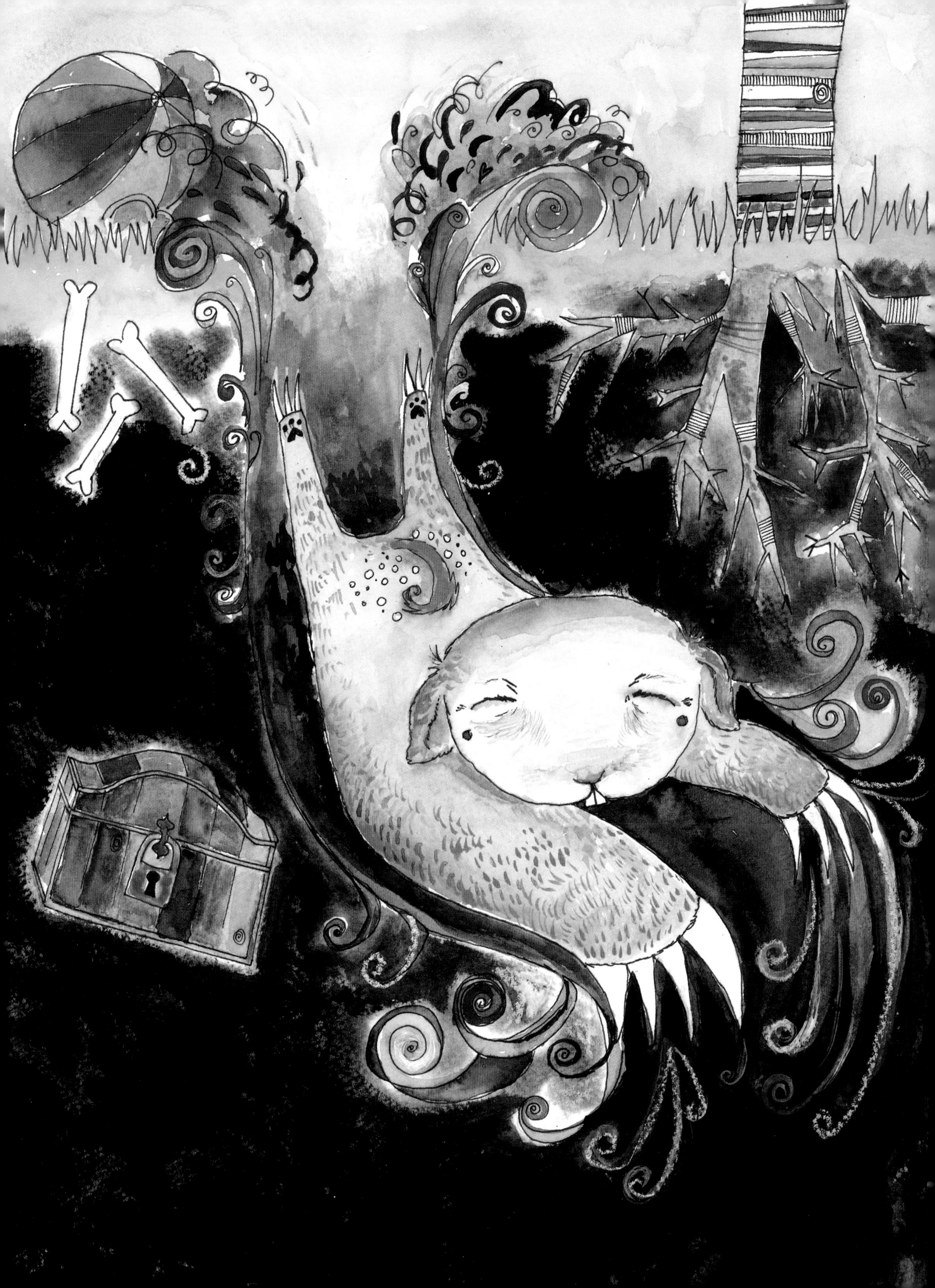

Right after I spotted him,
I climbed up and got him—
tied him up, but that didn't last long.

For, shortly thereafter,
I heard some dog laughter
and, once more, my Dizzy was gone!

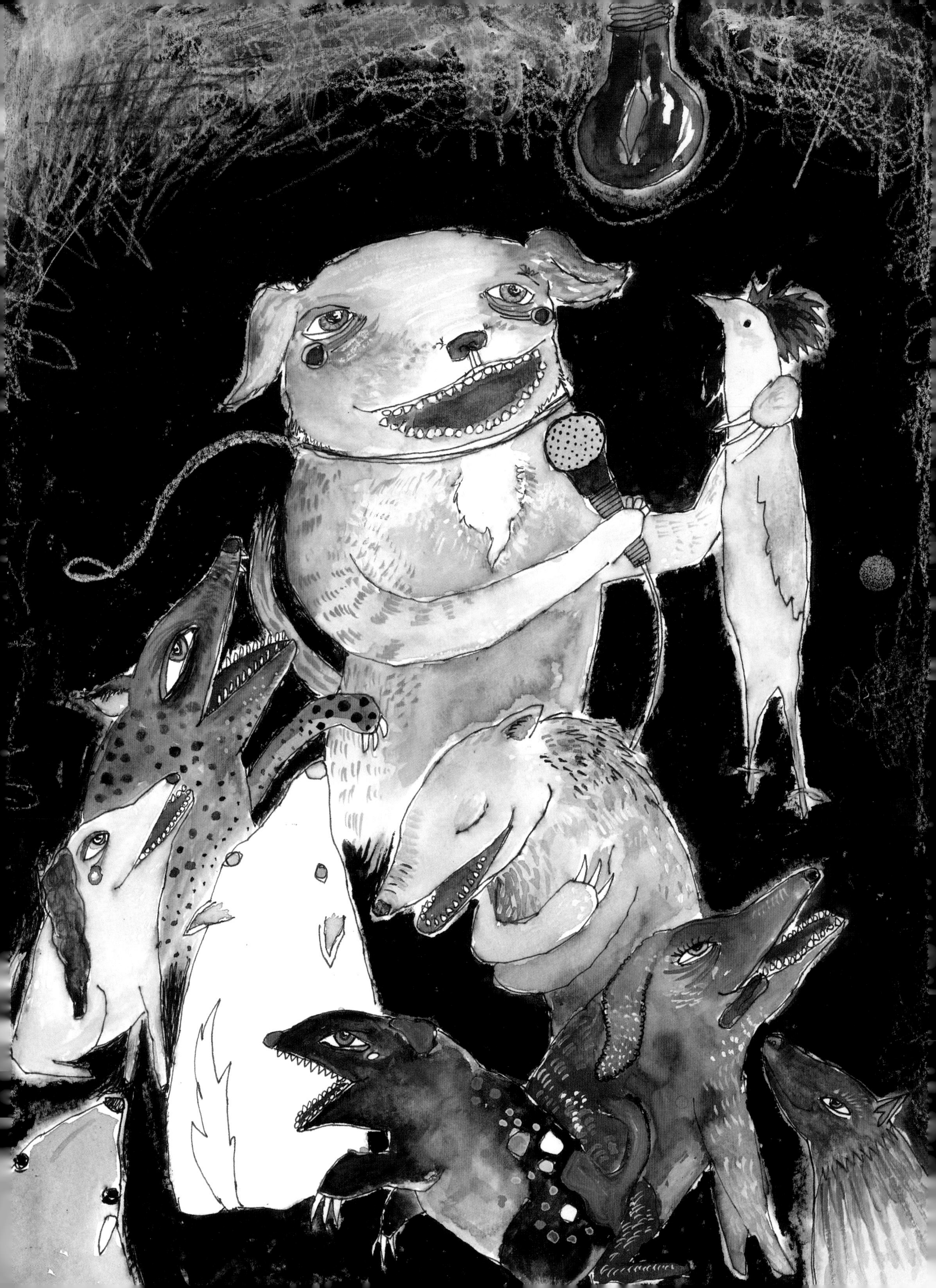

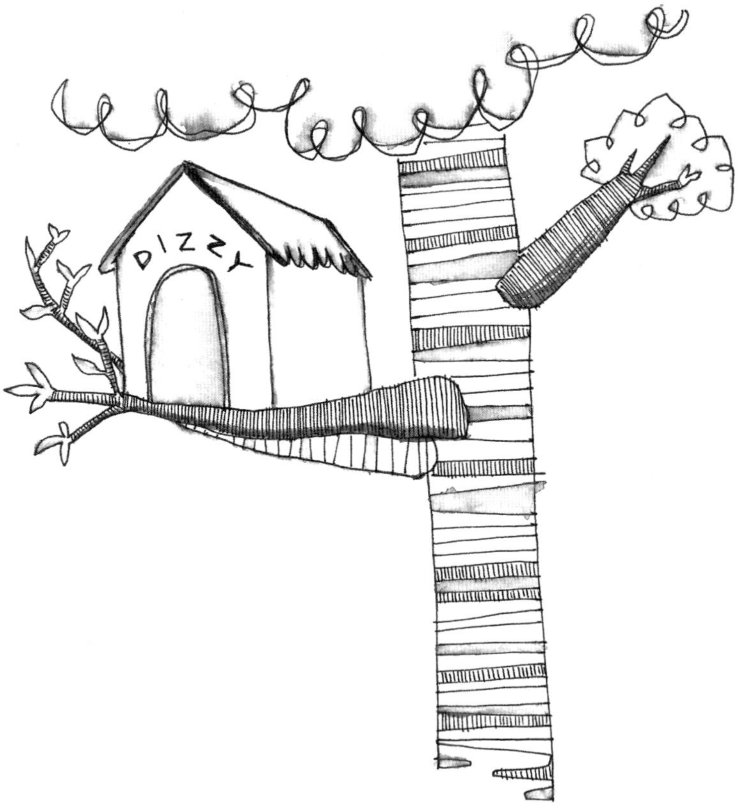
DIZZY

This time he got free
he was found in a tree,
though dogs don't know how to climb!

Is he part alley cat?
What else explains that?
How does Dizzy get out every time?

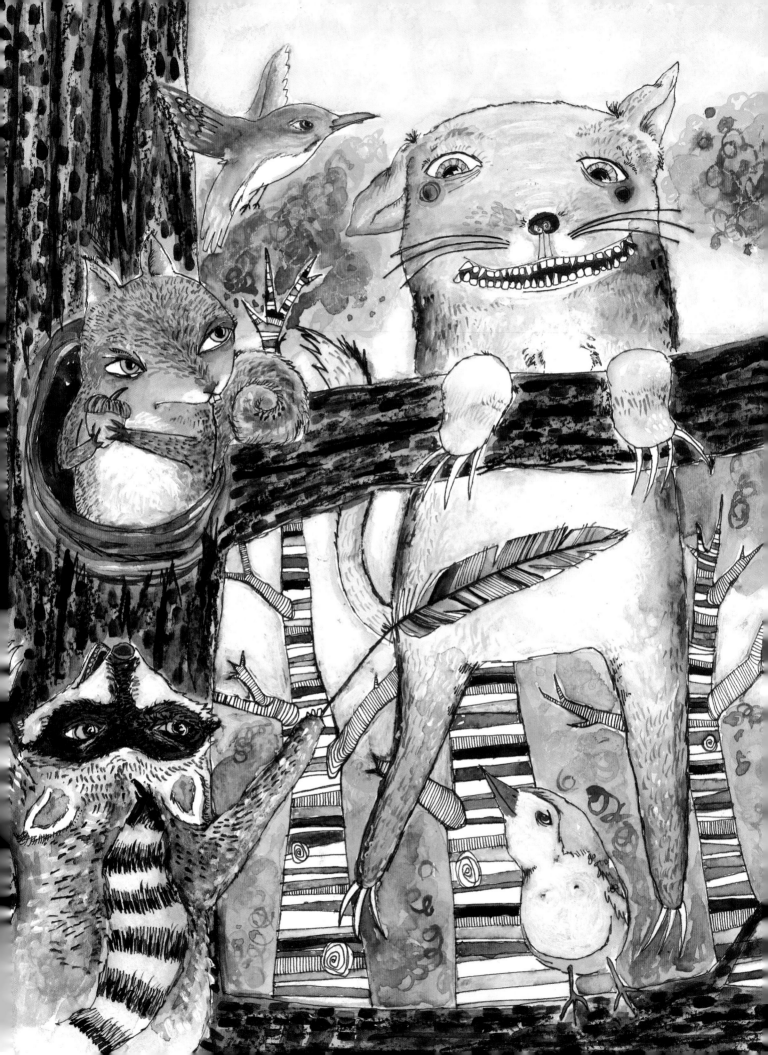

I was sort of half-furious
and kind of half-curious
to understand how Dizzy got loose.

For a moment or two,
I thought, "This dog flew!"
Could Dizzy be part poodle, part goose?

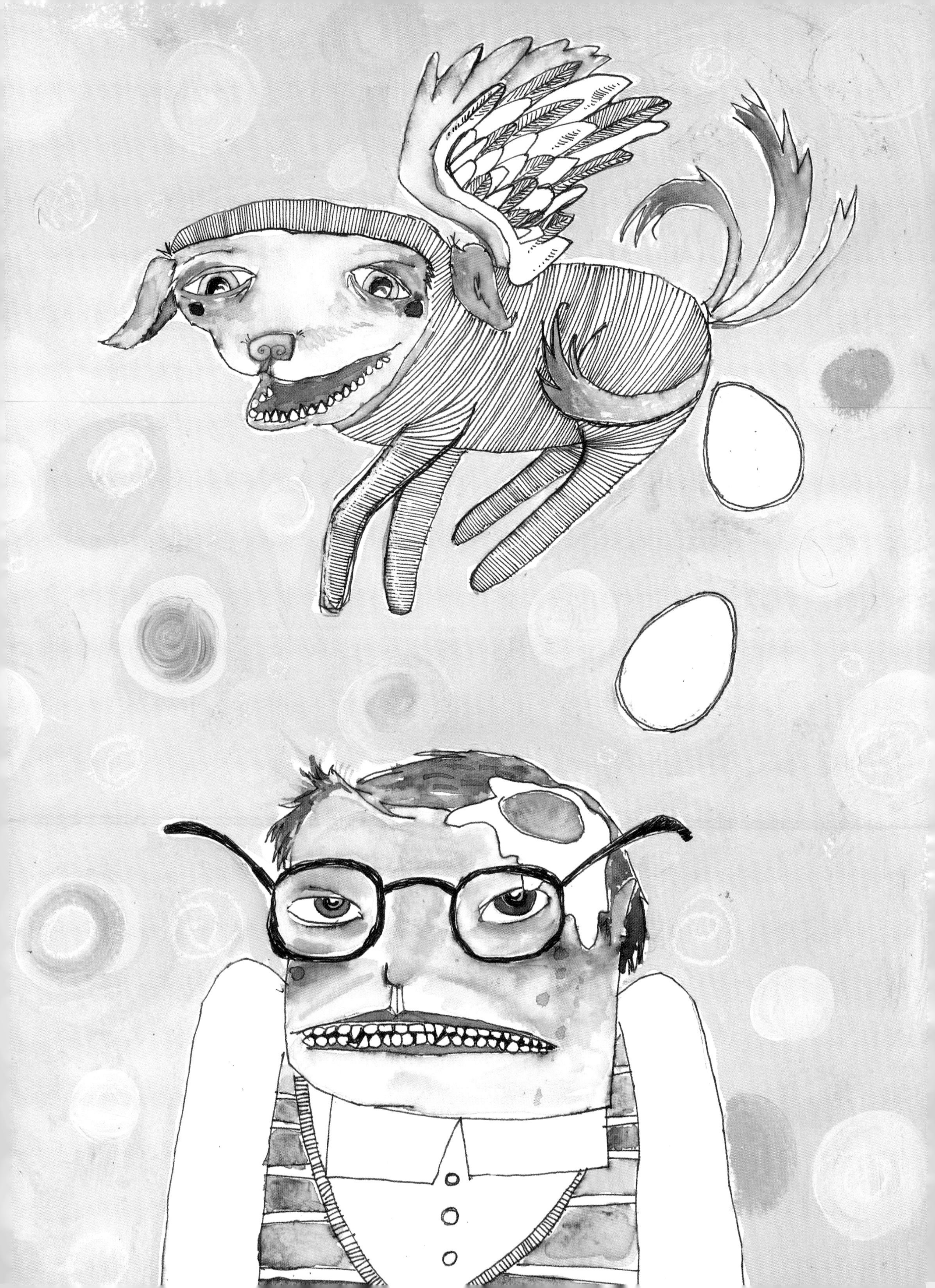

But he's **no flying** pup,
and I mustn't give up.
I had to control this lawn rover!

Oh, what an odd day!
He keeps getting away
past the fence—is it under or over?

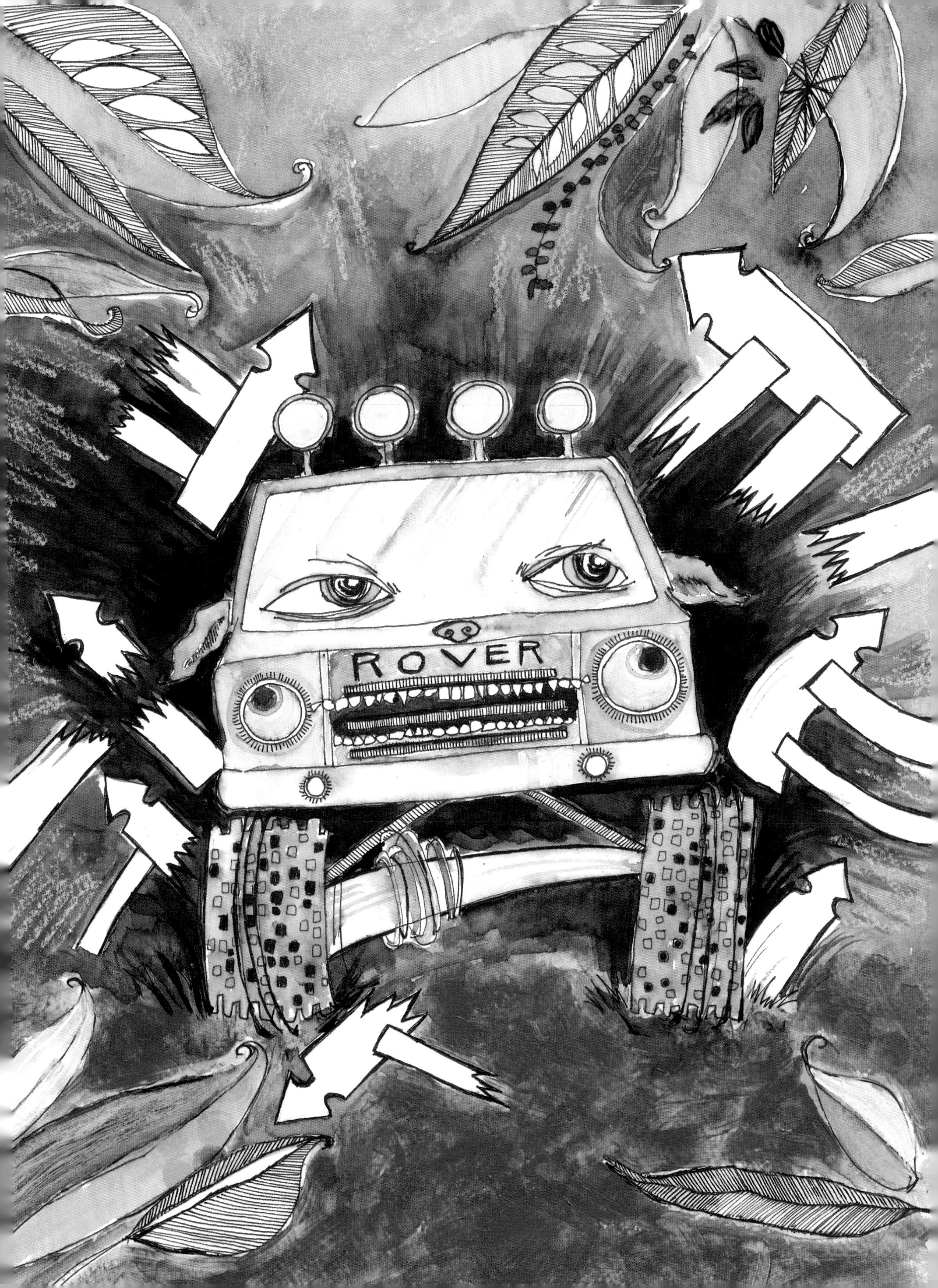
ROVER

So I tried extra hard
to Diz-proof the yard.
I covered every hole with wood.

All along the fence tops
I nailed sticks, rakes, and mops.
Get out? There's no way that he could!

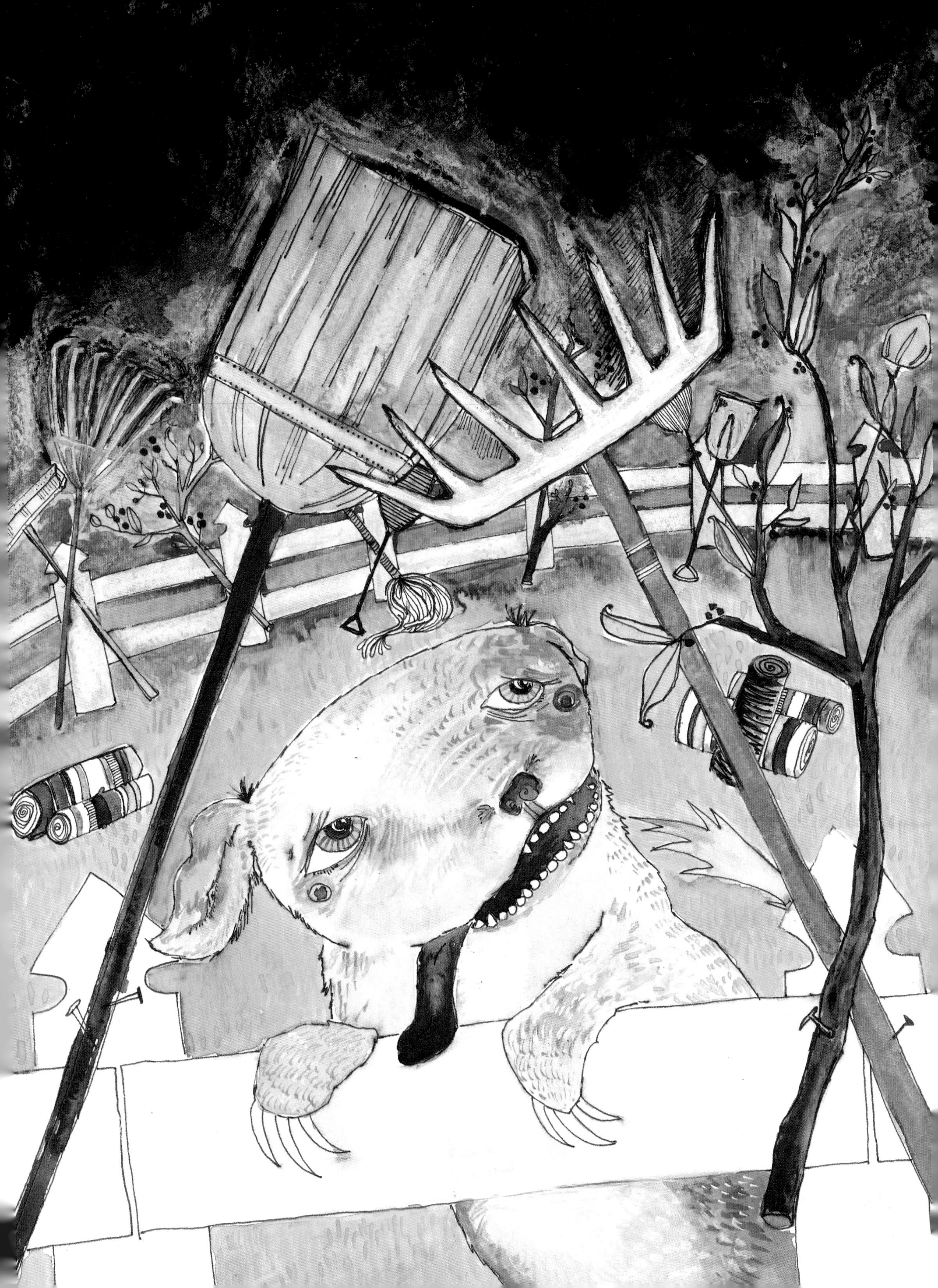

Then I went back inside,
very confident that I'd
finally managed to outsmart that Dizzy.

But in less than a minute,
our dog wasn't in it.
Our backyard was empty. Where is he?

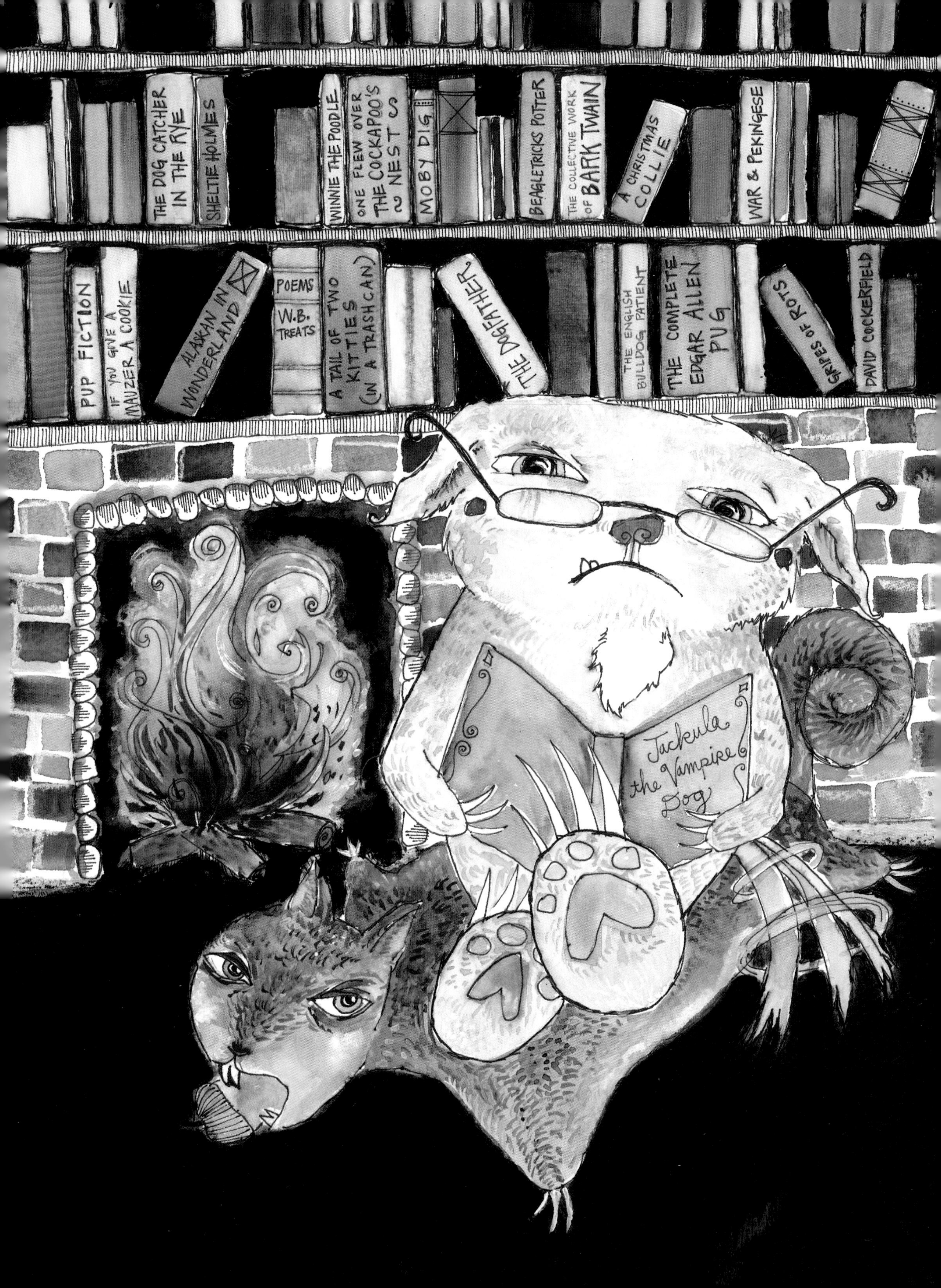
THE DOG CATCHER IN THE RYE
SHELTIE HOLMES
WINNIE THE POODLE
ONE FLEW OVER THE COCKAPOO'S NEST
MOBY DIG
BEAGLETRICKS POTTER
THE COLLECTIVE WORK OF BARK TWAIN
A CHRISTMAS COLLIE
WAR & PEKINGESE
PUP FICTION
IF YOU GIVE A MAUZER A COOKIE
ALASKAN IN WONDERLAND
POEMS
W.B. TREATS
A TAIL OF TWO KITTIES (IN A TRASHCAN)
THE DOGFATHER
THE ENGLISH BULLDOG PATIENT
THE COMPLETE EDGAR ALLEN PUG
GRIPES OF ROTS
DAVID COCKERFIELD
Jackula the Vampire Dog

"Hey, Dad," my boys said,
"He's upstairs on the bed."
There I found my boys rubbing his tummy.

Dizzy'd left his dog run,
and he'd had his dog fun,
and he fooled me like some kind of dummy.

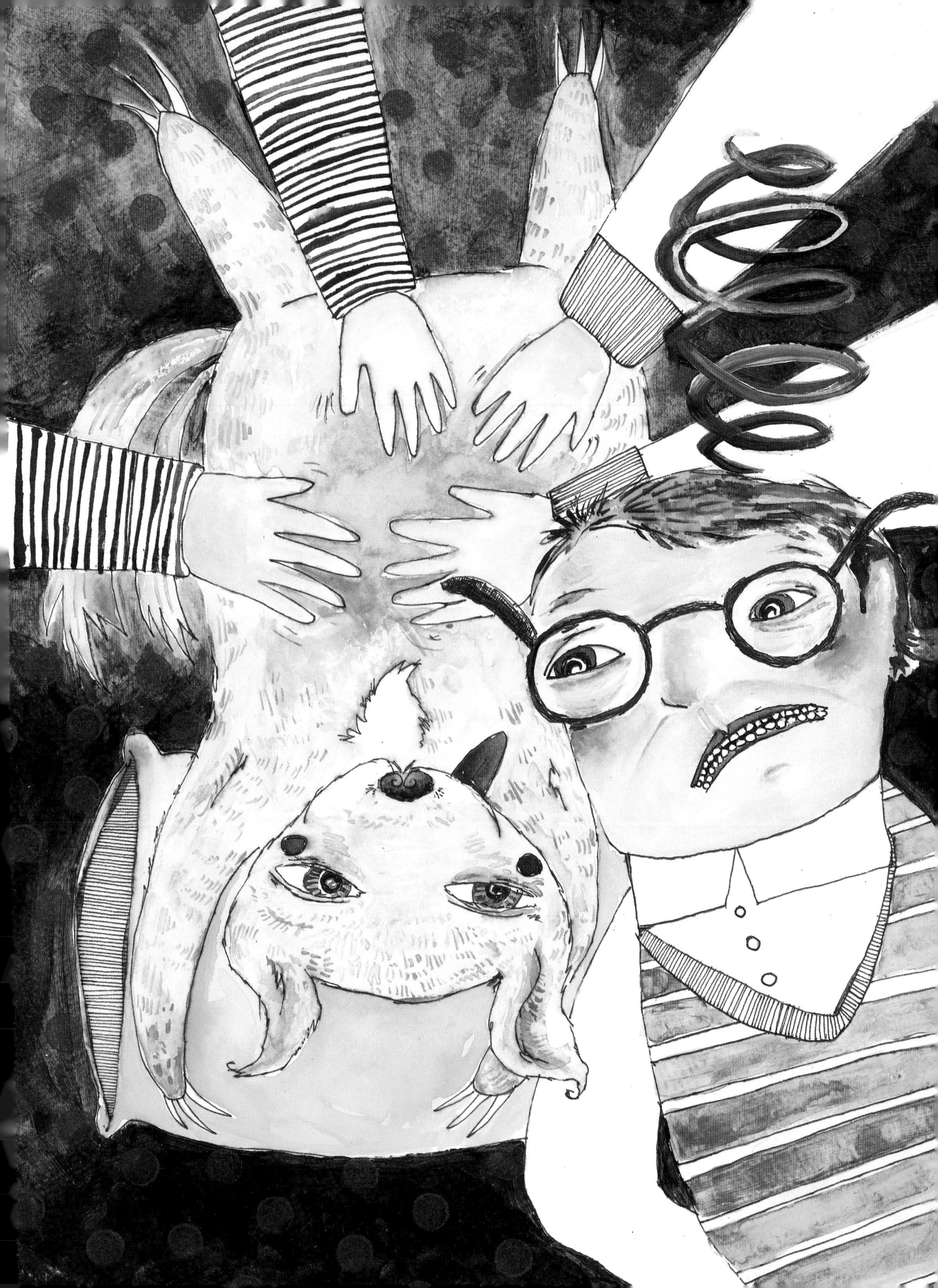

Part wizard, part poodle?
We're at the end of this doodle,
and for me it's not very clear.

Is he Dizzy the Mutt
with the Propeller Butt?
Hmmm? What's *your* answer, my dear?

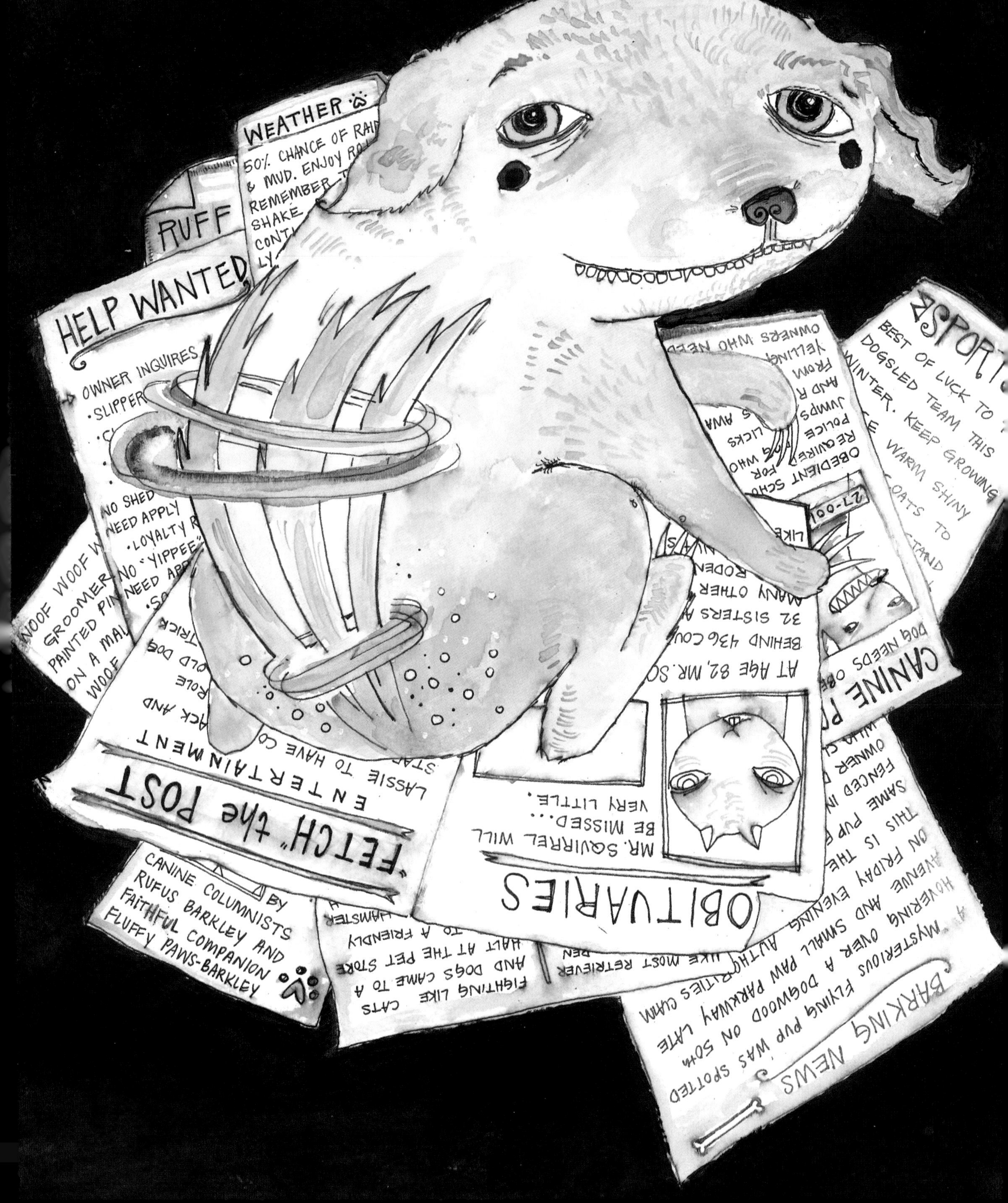

WEATHER
50% CHANCE OF RAI
& MUD. ENJOY RO
REMEMBER T
SHAKE
CONT
LY.
RUFF
HELP WANTED
OWNER INQUIRES
SLIPPER
NO SHED
NEED APPLY
LOYALTY R
NO "YIPPEE"
NEED APP
WOOF WOOF W
GROOMER
PAINTED PIN
ON A MAI
WOOF
SPORT
BEST OF LUCK TO
DOGSLED TEAM THIS
WINTER. KEEP GROWING
WARM SHINY
COATS TO
"FETCH" the POST
ENTERTAINMENT
LASSIE TO HAVE C
CANINE COLUMNISTS BY
RUFUS BARKLEY AND
FAITHFUL COMPANION
FLUFFY PAWS-BARKLEY
OBITUARIES
MR. SQUIRREL WILL
BE MISSED...
VERY LITTLE.
AT AGE 82, MR. SQ
BEHIND 436 COU
32 SISTERS A
MANY OTHER
OBEDIENT SCHO
FIGHTING LIKE CATS
AND DOGS CAME TO A
HALT AT THE PET STORE
TO A FRIENDLY
HAMSTER
CANINE
DOG NEEDS OBE
BARKING NEWS
A MYSTERIOUS FLYING PUP WAS SPOTTED
HOVERING OVER A DOGWOOD PARKWAY LATE
ON FRIDAY AND EVENING

Meet me

DizzyTheMutt.com

ISBN 10: 1-59298-328-6
ISBN 13: 978-1-59298-328-5

Library of Congress Control Number: 2010923343
Printed in the United States of America
First Printing: 2010
Second Printing: 2010

14 13 12 11 10   6 5 4 3 2

BEAVER'S POND
PRESS

Beaver's Pond Press, Inc.
7104 Ohms Lane, Suite 101
Edina, MN 55439-2129
(952) 829-8818
www.BeaversPondPress.com

To order, visit www.BeaversPondBooks.com
or call (800) 901-3480. Reseller discounts available.

Project management by Margery Punnett, Urban Cottage Company
Book design by Ryan Scheife, Mayfly Design (www.mayflydesign.net)

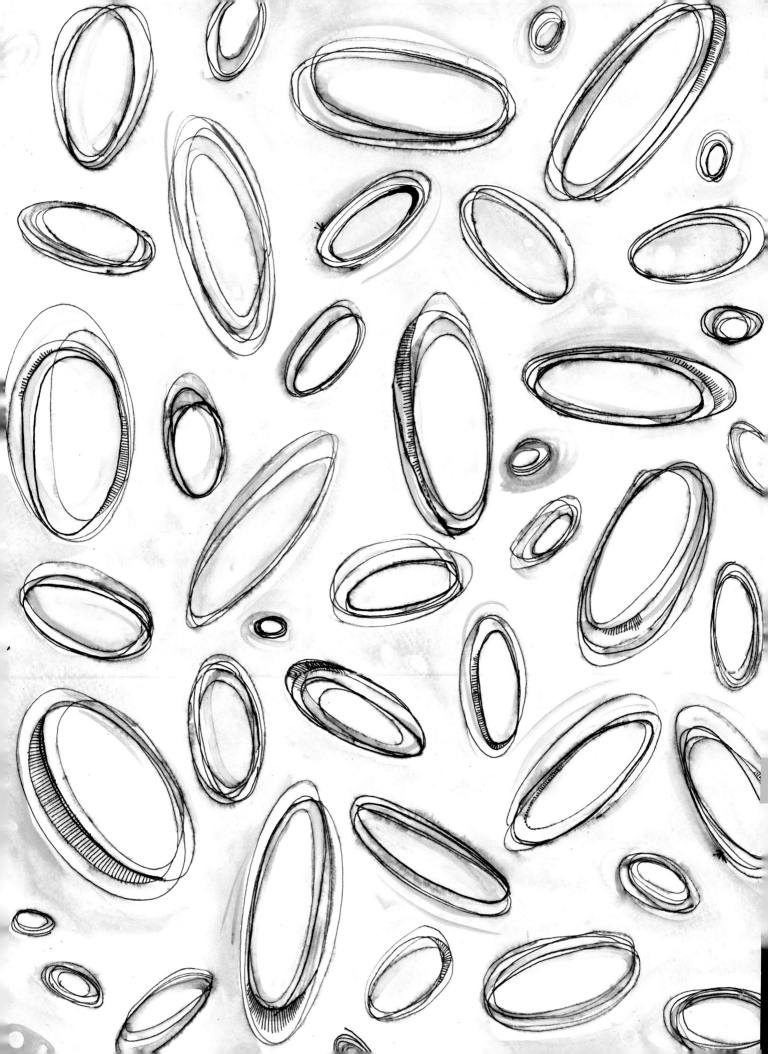